P
Ea

Easter alphabet

91-336

An Easter Alphabet

An Easter Alphabet

FROM A POEM BY

NORA TARLOW

with illustrations by
twenty-six artists
from the past

G. P. PUTNAM'S SONS   NEW YORK

Illustrations copyright © 1991 by Blue Lantern Studio
Text copyright © 1991 by G. P. Putnam's Sons
Primary text by Nora Cohen (Nora Tarlow).
All rights reserved. This book, or parts thereof,
may not be reproduced in any form without permission
in writing from the publisher.
G.P. Putnam's Sons, a division of
The Putnam & Grosset Book Group,
200 Madison Avenue, New York, NY 10016.
Published simultaneously in Canada.
Printed in Hong Kong by South China Printing Co. (1988) Ltd.
Book design by Kathleen Westray.
Library of Congress Cataloging-in-Publication Data.
An Easter alphabet/from a poem by Nora Tarlow:
illustrated by over twenty different
artists from the past. p. cm.
Summary: The letters of the alphabet introduce
the symbols and activities of Easter.
[1. Alphabet. 2. Easter – Fiction. 3. Stories in rhyme.]
I. Blue Lantern Studio.   PZ8.3.E129   1991
[E] – dc20   89-29376   CIP   AC

ISBN 0-399-22194-8

1 3 5 7 9 10 8 6 4 2

First Impression

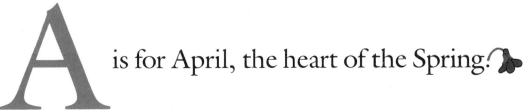

A is for April, the heart of the Spring.

B is for Bunnies and the Baskets they bring.

C is for Cart, with eggs piled upon it.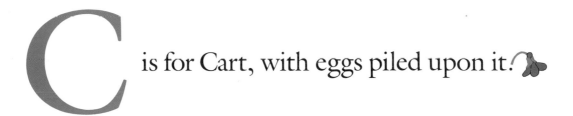

D is for Daisies we pick for our bonnets.

E is for Eggs, each a bright color.

F is for Family, sister and brother.

G is for Garden, hiding a treat.

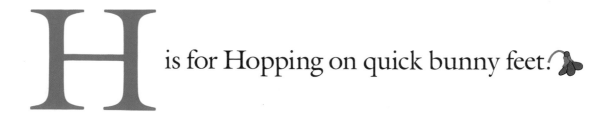

H is for Hopping on quick bunny feet.

I for Indoors, after egg-hunting ends.

J for the Joy we share with our friends.

K is for Kindness that makes the day bright.

L is for Lilies, lovely and white.

M is for Music we gather to play.

N is for Nest, filled with eggs the birds lay.

 for Outdoors, where we hunt by the hour.

P for the Puddles that follow a shower.

Q is for Quiet in the soft morning light.

R is for Rabbit, dressed up just right.

 is for Spring, when the world is in bloom.

T is for Tulips we place in each room.

U for Umbrella in sunshine or rain.

V is for Violets found in the lane.

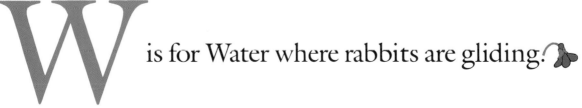
W is for Water where rabbits are gliding.

 X marks the spot where the eggs are hiding.

Y is for Young ones, happy at play.

Z is for Zeal as we greet Easter Day.

THE ARTISTS

THE END